Meet 100 Animals

Charles Doché

BALLOON BOOKS™

The gorilla is large and powerful, but only dangerous
if bothered. Even though it only eats fruits and leaves,
the male can weigh up to 600 pounds.

The chimpanzee is the closest living relative to humans. It eats mostly fruits and insects and can easily swing from tree to tree with its hands and feet.

The capuchin is a small, mischievous monkey that hangs from branches by its tail in the virgin forests of South America. It lives in small groups.

Squirrel monkeys have long tails and large eyes.
They live in South America, where they sleep in trees
by wrapping their tales around branches.

The kangaroo is an Australian mammal. The mother has a pouch where it carries its baby for the first six months of its life.

Another Australian animal, the koala bear, also has a pouch to protect its babies. Koalas eat three pounds of eucalyptus leaves a day!

Bats sleep during the day and come awake at night.
They are very helpful to gardeners because they eat
a lot of insects.

The hedgehog has sharp quills but is harmless. When it is scared, the hedgehog rolls into a ball. In winter, it sleeps beneath a pile of leaves.

Baby hares are able to hop just a few minutes after they are born. The hare has long ears and can move very quickly.

Rabbits are smaller than hares. In the wild they live in deep burrows in the ground. The rabbit eats roots, leaves, and vegetables.

Prairie dogs are members of the squirrel family. They get their name from their call, which sounds like a dog's bark. Prairie dogs kiss and groom each other.

Squirrels are found all around the world. There are
260 different species! Squirrels are excellent at
climbing and hopping from tree to tree.

Marmots are part of the squirrel family. They often sit upright to watch for danger. Marmots hibernate in deep tunnels for six months in the winter.

The beaver's flat tail makes it a very good swimmer. Its house is a dam built in the water out of branches and mud. These dams can last for many years.

The hamster is a popular pet. It eats seeds, fruits, and vegetables, which it can carry in pouches in each cheek.

Guinea pigs come from South America. It has small ears, short legs, and no tail. Many people keep guinea pigs as pets.

A dolphin is not a fish; it is a mammal. Dolphins are very playful and friendly, and also highly intelligent. They communicate with each other with sounds.

Foxes are members of the dog family. They have bushy tails and pointed ears and are very good hunters.

The wolf is a powerful and mysterious animal. He is a common character in Native American stories, where he is respected for his intelligence and grace.

Sheep dogs are a very smart dog breed. They help farmers round up sheep from the fields. The dingo, in the smaller picture, is a wild dog from Australia.

The brown bear is huge, and can be dangerous if bothered, but it mainly eats berries, insects, and small animals.

The polar bear is beautiful, but it will attack a human if it is hungry. It lives in the cold Arctic where it feeds on fish and seals.

The raccoon of North America is about the size of a cat. This busy animal washes its food, mainly fruits and plants, before it eats.

The panda bear has two black spots around its eyes.
It lives in China where it eats only bamboo leaves and
branches.

Otters can swim for a quarter mile under water before they have to come up for air. Though they have very short legs, on land they can run faster than humans.

During the day, the badger hides in a deep hole in the woods. It comes out at night to hunt insects, slugs and worms.

The wild cat prowls the woods during the night in search of birds, eggs, and mice. During the day it sleeps in trees.

These domestic cats are descendants of wild cats and, like their wild relatives, they also hunt birds and mice. They are independent and make very good pets.

The cheetah is the fastest land animal in the world. It can run as fast as 60 miles an hour—the speed of a car on a highway!

The tiger is the largest member of the cat family. It lives in the forests of Asia, where it hunts, prowls, and climbs trees. Unlike other cats, it sometimes swims.

A relative of the lion and tiger, the leopard is usually yellow with black spots. This allows him to hide in the tall grasses of Africa and Asia.

Powerful and proud, the lion is known as the "king of the beasts". It lives in packs in the vast, grassy plains of Africa.

The sea lion is a marine animal. It is very big but has tiny ears. The sea lion uses its flippers to move both in the water and on land.

Seals live mostly in cold bodies of water. They stay warm with a thick layer of fat under their skin. This also helps them float.

The African elephant has large ears and a powerful
trunk. It is the biggest and strongest land animal.
It lives on the plains.

The Indian elephant has smaller ears than its African cousin. It is often used for help with logging, due to its strong trunk.

The zebra's stripes allow it to hide from danger in the tall African grasses. Zebras sometimes form herds with other animals, such as antelopes.

The draft horse is large and robust. It is used as a work horse to pull plows and carts. These horses often have long manes and hair over their powerful hooves.

The saddlebred horse is lean and muscular and can carry a rider, run quickly, and jump high. It is the most common horse used in shows and competitions.

Ponies are much smaller than horses. Easy to feed and raise, they are often used to teach children how to ride.

Donkeys have been helping humans by carrying loads since 4000 BC! While donkeys have a reputation for being stubborn, they are actually very helpful.

The boar is an ancestor of the pig. It is very strong and lives in the wild, where it eats roots, insects, and rodents.

The rhinoceros is a dangerous giant. Because of its poor eyesight, it will attack things that move suddenly. But most of its time is spent grazing on grass.

The hippopotamus is dangerous only when it is bothered. It sleeps in the water during the day and eats grass on land at night.

The llama is the camel's cousin. It lives in herds in the mountains of South America, where its fur is used to make wool.

The camel stores fat in its humps which it can process into water. This allows it to survive in the desert. The dromedary, in the smaller picture, has only one hump.

A deer's antlers are shed each year and then grow back again! Deer live in herds in the forest and eat grass, twigs, and bark.

This species of very small deer is called a roe deer. At its highest it measures only 34 inches at the shoulder. When scared, the roe deer barks like a dog.

The ibex is a wild goat that lives on high mountain slopes. It is a master jumper and eats various kinds of grass. The male has long horns.

The goat produces milk, which is sometimes used to make cheese. Toy goats, in the smaller picture, are often kept as pets on farms.

The mouflon is a small wild sheep that lives in flocks. It eats grasses and leaves. The male has curved horns and a saddle-shaped mark on its back.

Sheep are raised mainly for their wool, which can be
spun to make fiber for sweaters and mittens.
A sheep's diet consists mostly of grasses.

The very rare okapi is a member of the giraffe family.
It lives in Africa, where it feeds on leaves and branches. The okapi was unknown to humans before 1900!

The giraffe is 13 to 16 feet tall. Its neck is long enough to reach leaves at the very tops of trees. No two giraffes have the same pattern on their coats.

The water buffalo is so strong that it can even attack a lion. It roams the African plains in herds, grazing on grass.

The bison is sometimes called a buffalo. It can weigh almost 2,000 pounds! Before the arrival of Europeans in America, there were as many as 50 million bison.

The highland cattle have lived for centuries in the harsh weather of Scotland. Despite their long horns, they are a very gentle breed.

Cows are common farm animals. In summer they graze on grass in the fields, and in winter they like to eat hay in the stable.

The impala, with its bent horns, is very swift and beautiful. It can leap up to 30 feet in length and 9 feet high. A member of the antelope family, it lives in Africa.

The gazelle is a quick and graceful member of the antelope family. Its stripes help it hide in the tall African grasses.

The blackbird is the jewel of gardens across Europe.
It eats worms, insects, and berries. The male bird is
black as its name suggests, but the female is brown.

With its red throat, the robin is easy to recognize.
People associate these little birds with the first signs of
spring.

The swallow is so swift it can capture insects in flight.
Its nest is made of mud. In fall, it migrates south.
Swallows are extremely graceful in flight.

The owl is a bird of prey that hunts mice and moles at night. The little owl, in the smaller picture, is a species of owl only eight inches long.

The female cuckoo lays an egg in the nest of another bird, often smaller, who will sit on it and later feed the hatched fledgling.

The parrot is a tropical bird that feeds on fruits and nuts. Some species can mimic human speech without understanding a single word.

The golden eagle captures small animals in woods or up in high mountains. It builds its nest on top of rocky cliffs.

Swans are often found in parks. They are very elegant animals. Their long necks allow them to reach plants on the bottom of ponds.

The wild duck is found on ponds and canals. The males are brightly colored, while the females are plainer in color, to help hide their babies.

The penguin lives in Antarctica. It can't fly, but is an excellent swimmer. Its diet consists of fish. The emperor penguin is the largest penguin.

The seagull eats worms, shellfish, and crabs. They are found both at sea and on land. They nest on dunes. There are approximately 47 species of gulls.

The pigeon is a grain-eater. Pigeons are often found in cities and parks. Some breeds have been trained to carry messages attached to their legs.

The ostrich is the largest bird on earth and is incapable of flying. The emu, in the smaller picture, cannot fly either. It is the second largest living bird.

Chickens can be found in the wild and on farms. There are many different breeds. The males tend to have brighter colors than the females.

Turtles have existed in the same form for over 200 million years! The sea turtle, in the smaller picture, comes onto land to lay eggs in the sand.

Crocodiles are extremely dangerous and will attack animals and humans with their swift, strong jaws. Its snout is longer than the alligator's.

All snakes are hunters. Some strangle their victims while others poison them. Certain species are dangerous to man.

Frogs catch worms, slugs, and insects. The green
frog, in the smaller picture, uses its color to hide in
ponds and swamps.

There are thousands of known species of fish. Some species, like the goldfish, are bred for pets. A goldfish is a freshwater fish.

Sharks never stop moving. They must swim constantly or else they will sink to the bottom of the ocean. They attack their prey with razor-sharp teeth.

Beetles have hard, protective wings. The may beetle destroys leaves and fruit. The borer beetle, in the smaller picture, will play dead when threatened.

The ladybug is a very useful insect to humans. It eats the aphids that invade garden plants. Most ladybugs are red or orange, spotted with black.

There are thousands of butterflies, of all colors and sizes. The flaming butterfly in the big picture. The red admiral butterfly, in the smaller picture.

The dragonfly often hovers, but it can also fly very quickly. It catches insects in flight and then carries them to be eaten on a plant.

The bee can be raised in hives by bee-keepers who collect their honey. A bee will die after stinging somebody.

Spiders are useful in catching insects. Some, like the garden spider, spin beautiful and intricate webs to catch their prey.

The lobster has a hard shell that protects it from predators. The lobster in the picture is a species that lives in tropical seas.

Earthworms live in the ground. In loosening the ground, they make it more fertile. They come out when it rains, to the delight of birds that feast upon them.

The garden snail has a soft skin that is protected by a shell. The stripes help it hide from its enemies. The Burgundy snail, in the smaller picture, is a brown color.

There is a countless number of shellfish in the seas.
People eat some shellfish, such as mussels or oysters.
The shells you find on beaches are from dead shellfish.

INDEX

Source of the illustrations: the pictures are from HR-Tierfoto and Diapress.